Henry,

your shadow will
always be your
friend

Clay A

The Lonely Shadow

by
Clay Rice

Green Pond Press

The Lonely Shadow

Published by Green Pond Press, LLC, Isle of Palms, South Carolina

Edited by Susan Kammeraad-Campbell
Book and jacket design by Steve Lepre
Photography by Liz Duren

1st Printing 2009
2nd Printing 2010
Printed in Mexico
A CIP catalog record for this book has been applied for from the Library of Congress.

ISBN 978-0-615-24900-1

DEDICATION

To the many children across this country for whom I've had the pleasure of creating "shadow pictures" over the past three decades.

To my wife Caroline; my son Charlie; and my son Connor, who was the inspiration and the model for the Lonely Shadow.

And to my Granddad, who taught me the art and magic of silhouettes when I was a little boy.

ACKNOWLEDGEMENTS

To Katherine Rice who, a long time ago, told me I could do anything I truly wanted to do.

To Steve Lepre. Thank you for your creativity and your genius.

The Lonely Shadow

Early one morning,
a little shadow
stood under a street lamp
and sighed.

"I am very lonely," he thought.

The shadow knew that he
belonged to someone,
he just didn't know who.

He thought, "If I could find my mate,
I would be very happy."

The little shadow went for a walk,
and while he walked he sang a song:

I have no you
you have no me,
you and me
we have no we,
but if I find you
and you find me,
happy we will always be.

The shadow stood by a door.

Am I a door?

He stood by a chair.

Am I a chair?

The shadow paused by an old man wearing polka dot underwear.

He looked high and he looked low,
but his mate did not show.

So the shadow kept walking
and while he walked, he sang:

I have no you
you have no me,
you and me
we have no we,
but if I find you
and you find me,
happy we will always be.

The little shadow went into the forest.

He dined with a deer.

He drank with a drake.

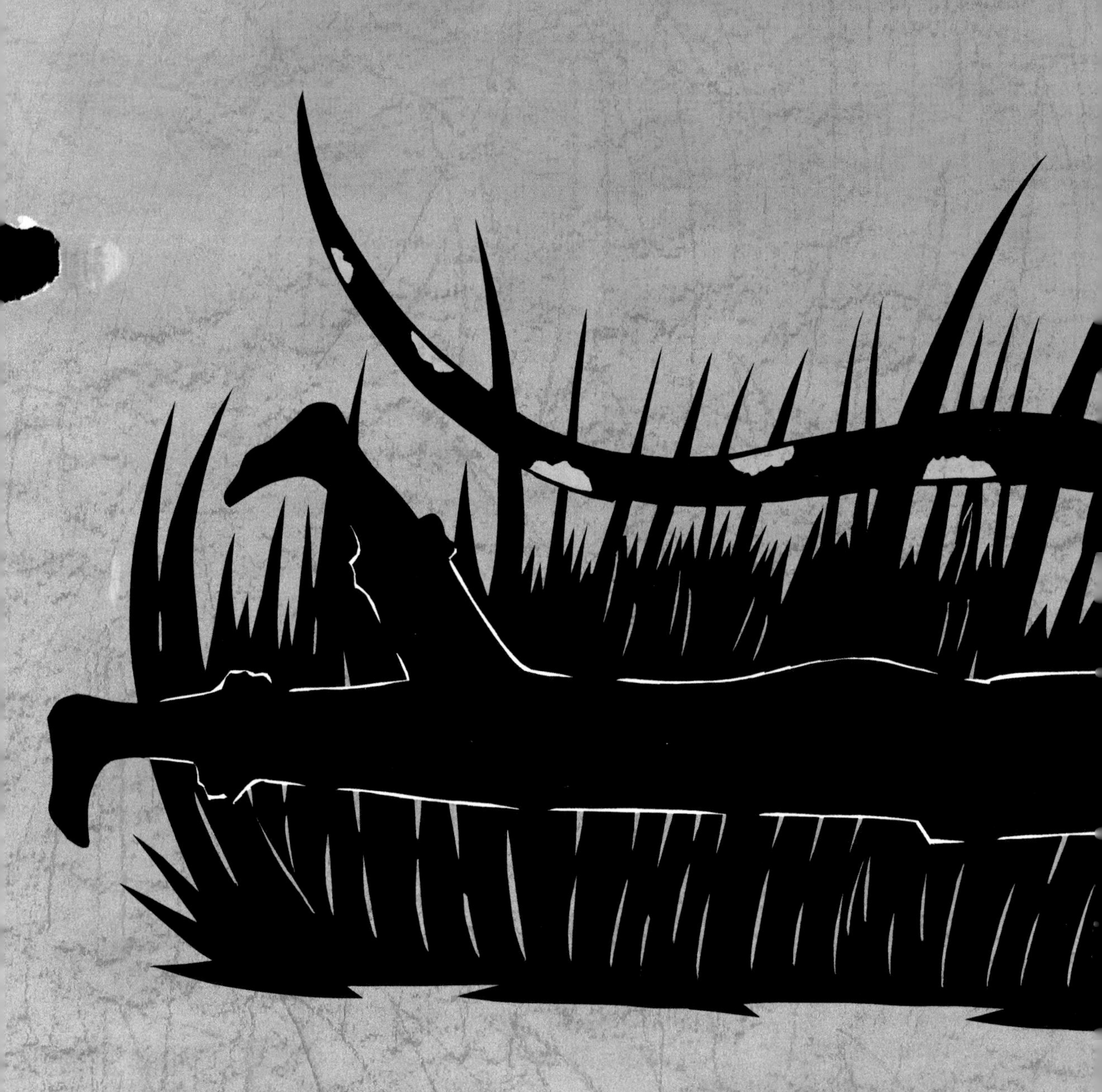

He stretched himself skinny and snuck with

snake.

But nowhere could
he find his mate.

He leaned against a tree.
He was very sad.
"If I could find my mate
how happy I would be."

Suddenly, a wise owl appeared.

"Don't be sad, little shadow," he said.
"You are just looking
in the wrong places.
You must go
where the children are."

This made the shadow happy.

He ran...and ran...
until he heard the sound of children
playing on the playground.

Evening was near
and many children and their shadows
were playing happily.

Then he saw a boy sitting all alone.

The little boy seemed sad.

The shadow walked up to the boy and asked, "Why are you so sad?"

The boy said, "It's late in the day, and that's when all the shadows come out to play. And I don't have one."

"I'll play with you,"
said the shadow.
"All right," said the boy.

They kicked a ball.

They streaked down a slide.

They jumped in a wagon and went for a ride.

They climbed a big tree.

They posed by a lake.

The bullfrog said "ribbit"
as they swam with the drake.

They slipped through the door.

They raced by the chair.

They pulled polka dots from
Grandpa's underwear.

And later that night as the
shadows grew long.

They took to the bed
as the big clock
went gong.

I have you,
you have me.
Together
we will always be.

About Silhouettes

by Clay Rice

More than 250 years ago a Frenchman named Silhouette thought it would be fun to cut out shadow shapes with scissors and black paper. He cut out shadow pictures of all of his friends and made cutouts to give as gifts.

Other artisits started making cutouts, too, and they called them silhouettes after the man who started the art form.

After all these years, only a few artists still make silhouette cutouts.

My grandfather, Carew Rice, was a silhouette artist. When I was a little boy, I loved watching him create beautiful picture cutouts. I started doing them, too. I've been doing them professionally for more than thirty years.